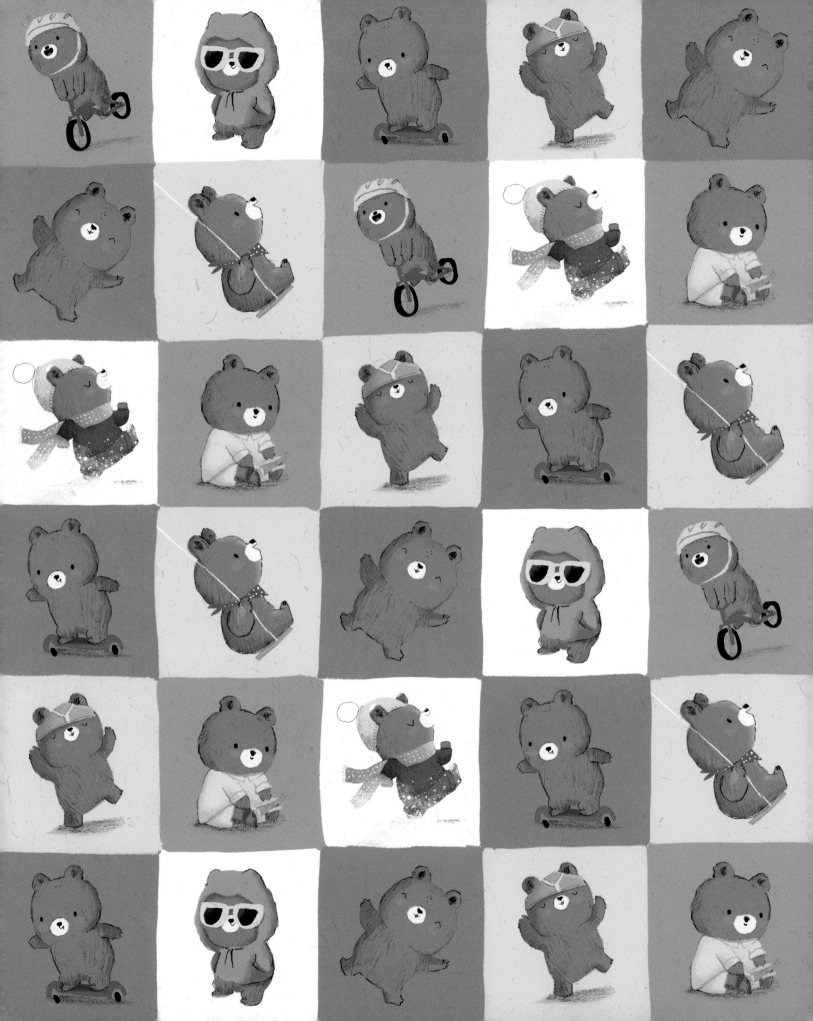

Willow Tree

A CIP catalogue record for this book is
available from the British Library

This edition published by Willow Tree Books, 2020
Willow Tree Books, Tide Mill Way, Woodbridge, Suffolk, IP12 1AP

0 2 4 6 8 9 7 5 3 1

Text © 2020 Willow Tree Books
Illustration © 2020 Willow Tree Books

Willow Tree Books and associated logos are trademarks and/or
registered trademarks of Imagine That Group Ltd

Written by Susie Linn
Illustrated by Alex Willmore

ISBN: 978-1-78958-577-3
Printed in China

www.willowtreebooks.net

For the Bear inside everyone. SL

Things I Love

by Bear
x

With help
from Susie Linn and
Alex Willmore

Here's a list of things I love.
They're things I want to share.
I've put them all inside this book
For you, with hugs from me, love Bear. x

This is me

My book

This book belongs to:

Bear

Bruno is my number one,
My best and bear-y friend.

Bruno

I love to run and play with him,
All day, until the very end.

Mummy runs my
bubble bath.
She fills it to the top.

Mummy

I love it when the bubbles float –
They wobble, shimmer,
shake and pop!

At bedtime Daddy reads to me.
He gives me lots of choice.

Daddy

I love to pick the funny books,
And giggle when he does each voice.

Grandpa Bear is so much fun.
He sometimes comes to stay.
I love it when he lets me win,
And miss him when
he goes away.

Grandpa

Bear hugs
are the
BEST!

I'm a bear, a furry bear,
I love to be all snug,
And wrapped up safe in Mummy's arms,
A cosy, shaggy, big bear hug!

I love see-saws, slides and bars,
But more than all of these,

I love to swing above the park,
High up, above the tallest trees.

When golden leaves begin to fall
And drift down to the ground,

I really cannot help myself –
I love to roll and roll around.

On winter days of
cold and sun,
And snowflakes
on my nose,

I love to stomp in
snowy drifts,
And scrunch the snow
between my toes.

I love to ride upon my bike
And do some awesome tricks.

I balance on the handlebars,
Or juggle with a pile of sticks.

I'm not like all the other bears.
I really don't know why.

HONEY

Although I quite like honey,
I LOVE ice cream and apple pie!

I love to wear my underpants,
Not where they should belong.
I wear them on my head instead!
I know it looks so very wrong!

The thing that makes me laugh the most –
I cry, I just can't stop –

I love the funny, squeaky sound
Of my friend Bruno's windypops.

I love the naughty little voice
That whispers in my ear.
It tells me silly jokes to play –
Be bear-y wary, DON'T come near!

AH-CHOO!

My birthday's soon – I cannot wait!
I hope I don't sound rude.

I really do love birthday gifts,

And yummy birthday
party food.

I sometimes dress up,
clean and smart.
It makes my mummy proud.

But hoody tops are
what I love –

I AM the coolest bear around!

I love to look at things so small,
Like leaping, hopping bugs.
I even love to look up close
At icky-sticky, slimy slugs!

On windy days,
all whoosh and blow,
I love to fly my kite.

I throw it high into the air
And watch it soar up, out of sight.

On rainy days it pours and pours,
But I don't really mind.

I love to keep my PJs on
And play with toys of every kind.

Although I am a brave, strong bear,
I love a paw to hold.
I think, maybe, I always will,
Even when I'm very old!

I am a lucky bear, I know,
As Daddy's always there.
I love that I can tell him things,
Any time or anywhere.

Now you know the things I love,
How much I really care.

If you have things to
share with me,
Please whisper them.

With love from Bear.

x